Two Christmas Mice

by **Corinne Demas**

illustrated by **Stephanie Roth**

Holiday House / New York

Text copyright © 2005 by Corinne Demas
Illustrations copyright © 2005 by Stephanie Roth
All Rights Reserved
Printed in the United States of America
www.holidayhouse.com
First Edition
1 3 5 7 9 10 8 6 4 2

Library of Congress Cataloging-in-Publication Data
Demas, Corinne.
Two Christmas mice / written by Corinne Demas; illustrated by Stephanie Roth.
p. cm.
Summary: Two mice, who discover they are neighbors, bring their talents together
to create a very special Christmas tree.
ISBN 0-8234-1785-9 (hardcover)
[1. Christmas—Fiction. 2. Mice—Fiction. 3. Christmas trees—Fiction.
4. Neighbors—Fiction.]
I. Roth, Stephanie, ill. II. Title.
PZ7.D39145Tw 2003
[E]—dc21
2002192231
ISBN-13: 978-0-8234-1785-8
ISBN-10: 0-8234-1785-9

For my goddaughter,
Hadley
C. D.

To my parents,
Marlies and Brian
S. R.

IT WAS THE MORNING BEFORE CHRISTMAS. Annamouse, who lived in the hay field south of Big Maple Tree, was setting up her Christmas tree in her parlor. First it wibble-wobbled to the right. Then it wibble-wobbled to the left. Finally it stood up straight.

Willamouse, who lived in the hay field north of Big Maple Tree, was making paper chains. First the glue wasn't sticky enough. Then it was too sticky. Finally it was just right.

By afternoon it had started snowing. It snowed and it snowed. Annamouse got ready to go to town to buy decorations for her Christmas tree. But when she got to the end of her long burrow, the snow was too deep. She closed her door tight.

Willamouse got ready to go to town to buy her Christmas tree. But when she got to the end of her long burrow, the snow was too deep. She closed her door tight.

What was Annamouse going to do without decorations for her tree? Would Santamouse even know it was a Christmas tree?

Annamouse found an old pie tin in the pantry and cut out a
silver star. She put it on top of the tree.

What was Willamouse going to do without a Christmas tree?

Willamouse took her cape and bonnet off the coatrack in the hall. Then she dragged the coatrack down the burrow to her parlor.

She stood the coatrack up in the corner. Would Santamouse know it was supposed to be a Christmas tree? She decorated it with the paper chains.

Annamouse ate a little supper and hoped it would stop snowing. She'd planned to go caroling with all the other mice from the south hay field. They always sang to the rabbits who lived in the blackberry patch since, as you know, rabbits are fond of carols but can't sing at all.

But when Annamouse looked out, the snow was even deeper. The wind blew snow right into her tidy front hall. She had to push hard to close the door tight. All alone on Christmas Eve. And no caroling!

This was Willamouse's first Christmas in her new home. She ate a little supper and hoped it would stop snowing. She'd planned to go caroling with all the other mice from the north hay field. They sang to the squirrels at the edge of the woods since, as you know, squirrels are fond of carols but can never remember the words.

But when Willamouse looked out, the snow was even deeper. The wind blew snow all over her cape and bonnet. She had to push hard to close the door tight. All alone on Christmas Eve. And no caroling!

Annamouse got her violin from her music room. At least she'd play some Christmas music by her tree. She hung her portrait of Mouzart, her favorite composer, on the parlor wall for company.

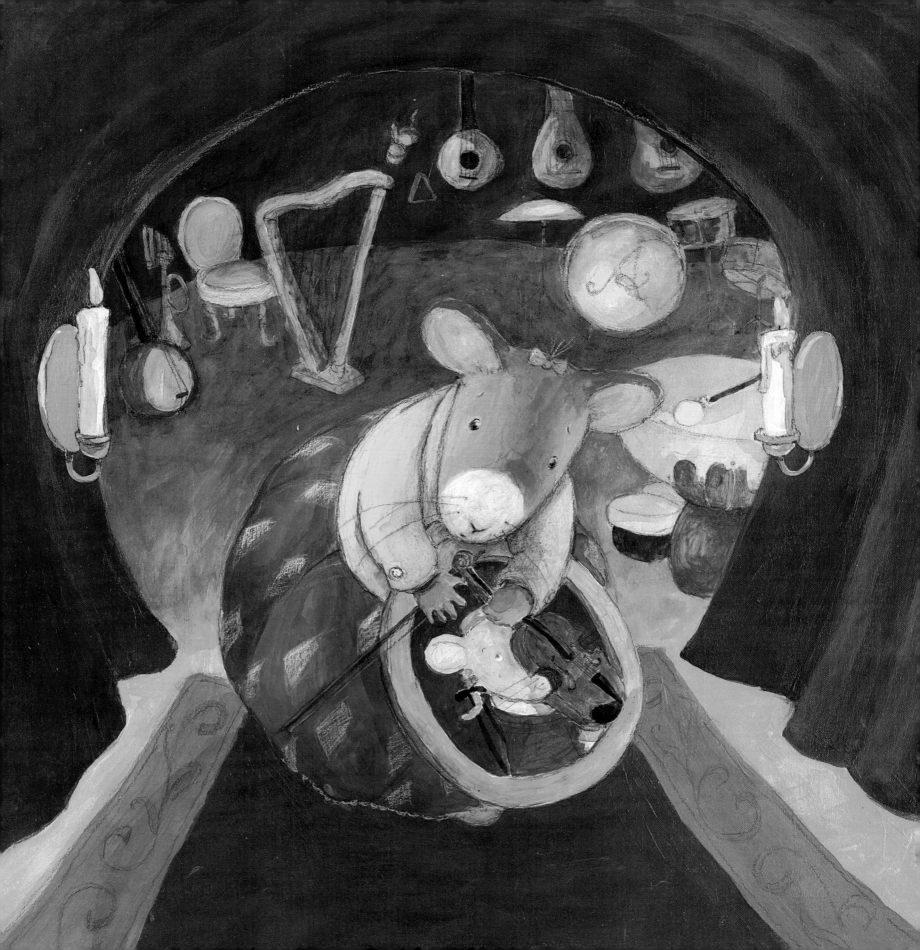

Willamouse curled up on her soft sofa. It was the first time she'd sat in her parlor since she moved in. She decided to read aloud from *The Night Before Christmas*.

"'Twas the night before Christmas,
    when all through the house
    Not a creature was stirring . . ."

But something *was* stirring. Willamouse looked up from her book. Something was happening on the other side of the parlor wall. But that couldn't be.

Willamouse started reading again.

"Not a creature was stirring, not even a mouse."

But now there was no mistaking it. First there were some odd notes. Then there was music. It was coming from right behind her portrait of Mouzart, her favorite composer.

Willamouse stood close to the portrait of Mouzart. Someone was playing Christmas carols on a violin. Willamouse lifted the portrait down and pressed her ear against the wall. Only a mouse could play that well. She tapped on the wall, but no one answered. She tapped again, louder. Then she knocked with both paws. Still no answer.

She spread some newspaper on the floor and started to dig.

Annamouse finished playing "Silent Night." But it wasn't a silent night at all. There was an odd scratching sound coming from the wall of her parlor, right behind her portrait of Mouzart.

Annamouse put down her violin and pressed her ear against the wall. It sounded like digging.

Annamouse lifted the portrait of Mouzart off the wall. There was a hole in the wall. And peering through the hole was a friendly mouse face. It was Willamouse!

Although the front doors of Annamouse's burrow and Willamouse's burrow were far apart in different hay fields, their parlors were actually close together. Annamouse and Willamouse were neighbors, but they had never seen each other before.

"A new friend for Christmas!" cried Willamouse.

"Let's take down the whole wall!" cried Annamouse.

So they did.

Soon they had one big parlor with two fireplaces. They swept up the mess and put Annamouse's tree in the center of the room. They strung it with Willamouse's beautiful paper chains. The tree looked perfect.

Annamouse and Willamouse stayed up late, dancing around the tree and singing carols. "Fa la la la la."

Then they fell asleep on Willamouse's soft sofa. And just in time. For Santamouse had arrived. He slid down Annamouse's chimney and found that he was in Willamouse's parlor too. He piled their presents under the tree.

To: Annamouse and Willamouse

Annamouse and Willamouse are both still asleep. But since you are curious, here is what Santamouse brought them. Annamouse will get a silver violin charm on a pink silk ribbon. Willamouse will get a pink diary with a purple plume pen. And inside the big box with both of their names on it is a china tea set for two.